Shine On, Butter-Finger

*To Ramadhin and Valentine
and to the stick fighters and calypsonians,
griots of word and movement*

Shine On, Butter-Finger copyright © Frances Lincoln Limited 2007
Text copyright © Bob Cattell and John Agard 2007
Illustrations copyright © Pam Smy 2007

First published in Great Britain and the USA in 2007 by
Frances Lincoln Children's Books, 4 Torriano Mews,
Torriano Avenue, London NW5 2RZ
www.franceslincoln.com

Distributed in the USA by Publishers Group West

British Library Cataloguing in Publication Data
available on request

ISBN 978-1-84507-626-9

Printed and bound in Great Britain by
Mackays of Chatham

1 3 5 7 9 8 6 4 2

Shine On, Butter-Finger

Bob Cattell and John Agard

Illustrated by Pam Smy

F

FRANCES LINCOLN
CHILDREN'S BOOKS

Chapter 1

Sitting astride the heavy roller, Riccardo swung his feet and scribbled in his song book. The sun had dipped below the palm trees by the pavilion; the singing of the cicadas grew louder and louder and mosquitoes droned past his ears. He had only a few minutes left to finish his poem before the meeting started. And anyway it would soon be too dark to see. Night came swiftly in the islands.

> Evening come
> With evening sun;
>
> Sunset gold
> In palm tree crown...

It was a moody sort of poem, a poem with a sad evening feeling. His red song book was almost full, crammed with all the things he had written: reggae and soca, sad songs and funny poems that played with words the way Riccardo loved. Then there were what he called his 'angry songs', rants about the things that bothered him, and of course the calypsos. But he hadn't written a calypso for several weeks. They just weren't coming out of his head any more... and that was a problem, because in less than two weeks he'd be on stage at the Calypso Monarch Final.

The invitation had arrived a few days earlier.

Official invitation to Riccardo Small to compete in the Calypso Monarch Final at Constantine Bay, it began. The white card was printed in raised black letters, except for the words 'Riccardo Small' which had been written by hand in a fine, curly script.

At first he fancied it was some sort of joke – somebody at *Calypso Cricket Club* making fun of him. But as he read the letter over and over, he knew it was for real. He, Riccardo Small, had been chosen to take part in the annual calypso competition, the biggest event of the whole year. And his first thought was to tell Count Crawfish.

Crawfish was the most famous singer on the Island. He was the only person ever to win three Calypso Finals in a row. Riccardo had never met anyone like him. He worked as the groundsman at the Oval cricket ground where the Island first team played. With his long wispy white beard and wrinkled face, Count Crawfish could have been taken for a priest or some ancient mariner, but his bright eyes sparkled like a child's when he sang. He'd spotted Riccardo's poetic talent the moment they met, and since that first chance encounter, the young boy and the old calypsonian had become firm friends.

Crawfish was jubilant when Riccardo told him about the invitation. "Young Rikki Tikki off to Calypso War," he said, a broad smile flickering across his weather-beaten face. "So why, in heaven name, you look so 'fraid?"

"'Cos I don't know what to do."

"Do? What you think you do, Riccardo? Sing, of course."

"But what shall I sing?"

"Sing your sweet songs," said Crawfish. Then, more helpfully, he painted a picture of the Final for Riccardo. Every year during Carnival, the Count told him, five calypsonians fought for the title of 'Calypso Monarch' at Constantine Bay. From all over the Island the villagers came to cheer on their champions and there were tents and stalls and bands playing. "Each contestant sing two new calypsos," said the Count. "They write them special for the Final and they judged on their songs and their performance too."

"And what they about?" asked Riccardo.

"Anything under the sun. But the crowd always appreciate a song that make them laugh or cry."

"Five singers? Who the other four?"

"No one tell me yet. The Growling Pantha there, for sure – he the reigning Monarch. And Diabolo, who seeking revenge 'cause he say Pantha steal his crown."

Riccardo had never heard the Growling Pantha sing live but his songs were played everywhere – blasting out from the bars and the store-fronts and in the minibuses. Once Uncle Alvin had taken him to see Diabolo perform. They hadn't enjoyed it much. It wasn't the songs Riccardo didn't like but the way Diabolo sang them. "That boy too damn arrogant," Uncle Alvin had said. "I know his father, André Ally. He come from Five Roads, sugar plantation village on Atlantic side. He ain't no good either."

"Chutney singer, Roti Boy most likely be there, too," added the Count.

"But they all famous," protested Riccardo.

"Famous? What that mean?" said the Count. "I tell you 'bout fame." And he tapped out a rhythm on his lunch box as he sang this song:

The slower ball, the slower ball
Does deceive batsman and make wicket fall.
Before you walk, before you walk,
Count Crawfish say first learn how to crawl.

So take it slow up the ladder of fame,
Don't mind the paper, them praising your name.
Today they raise you up to the limelight,
Tomorrow you forgotten and out of sight.

People, take this advice from the Count,
When you climb fame ladder, mind how you mount.
Remember how the slower ball does hit the bail
And the higher monkey go, the more he show he tail.

Count Crawfish threw his head back and laughed.

"Fame, man, you no need to worry 'bout that. Pantha, Diabolo, they the ones under pressure. No one expect you to win. So you go and enjoy your day."

The fireflies were dancing over the cricket ground as Riccardo finished his poem. Like all the other songs, the words had come into his head and he'd written them down. Later he'd work on it again until the rhythms were just right. He hummed the tune of the ballad – if only it had been a calypso – and then his voice drifted across the empty cricket ground.

> Evening come
> With evening sun;
>
> Sunset gold
> In palm tree crown;
>
> Hibiscus now
> Is closed up flower;
>
> Darkness hums,
> The firefly hour.
>
> Sleep, island,
> Dream sea-water dream.

A rumble of sound from the pavilion brought him back to the present. The meeting was about to start. He stuffed the red book and pencil into his back pocket and jumped down from the roller.

Calypso's cricket pavilion was bursting at the seams. Natty had called 'a very important meeting' and everyone was there – all the players and the musicians too. *Calypso CC* was the only cricket club on the Island with a full calypso band, and the band and the the team were inseparable. Waiting for the proceedings to begin, Ram the bongo player and the two steel guitars led the others in an improvised tune.

◎ ◎ ◎

The band was one of the reasons why Riccardo loved *Calypso CC* so much. It was the best cricket club in the whole wide world. Better than the famous *MCC* at Lord's, even – because he was pretty sure they didn't have a band. He saw Bashy and pushed his way through the bodies towards him, greeting all his friends as he went.

"Where you been?" asked Bashy.

"Nowhere special. What going on?"

"Don't know. Natty keeping it a secret," said

Bashy. "I ask him what it all about but he say sorry, Bash, you have to wait just like all the rest."

"Season over," said Riccardo. "What can it be that so important?"

"Big Lug say we going to make movie about we famous victory," said Bashy with a grin. "If it a musical you can sing all your songs."

"Take no notice of Big Lug," said Riccardo. "He always talk nonsense."

Big Lug was Leo, the team's lightning fast bowler – the nickname came from his sticking-out ears. The victory Bashy spoke of was the greatest game in the history of *Calypso CC*. They had triumphed over the mighty *Windward Wanderers* in the final of the Cup and everyone on the Island was still talking about that remarkable day – about how Leo and Natty had bowled *Calypso* back into the game and Bashy's great rescue innings and Leo, of all people, scoring the winning runs.

But mainly they were talking about Riccardo – Little Riccardo who they said wasn't good enough to play for the team because he couldn't bat and he couldn't bowl, but most of all he couldn't catch. They called him Butter-Finger. But it was Butter-Finger who sang *Calypso* to its sweetest victory. Riccardo's calypsos had inspired his team – turned the game around when all seemed lost. That's why everyone on the Island knew Butter-Finger's name and no one, except Riccardo himself, had been surprised that he'd been chosen for the Calypso Final.

Bashy, *Calypso*'s wicketkeeper, was Riccardo's best friend. Riccardo's Uncle Alvin said Bashy would play for the West Indies one day. "Most talented young cricketer I come across since I first see young Brian Lara," he'd say. Riccardo would have done anything to play cricket like Bashy. And Bashy would have given away his cricket bat to sing like Riccardo.

"C'mon, Natty," boomed Leo. "We in suspense long enough. Tell us what it all about, man."

"OK, quiet down and I tell you," said Natty. Natty had been captain of *Calypso* for two years. He was a fine all-rounder, immensely popular with all the players. The musicians stopped playing and everyone listened.

"We got a big game coming," began Natty, putting on his most serious expression.

"Who we playing?" demanded Leo.

"Can't you keep quiet one minute, Big Lug?" shouted someone.

"Game against *Grand Bay Cricket Club*," said

Natty, ignoring the interruption.

"*Grand Bay*? Never heard of they. Where they from?" asked Desmond, the opening batter.

"From Carriacou."

"Carriacou?" everyone chorused.

"Why we want to play Carriacou team?" demanded Leo.

"We playing them in the Valentine Shield," said Natty quietly. A buzz went round the pavilion. The Valentine Shield – it was the biggest junior club cricket trophy in all the islands. All the top West Indian teams had played in it. The Shield competition took place every year in Trinidad. "We entered because we win the Cup," explained Natty. "First we play in the qualifying round – here at the Oval Cricket Ground – 'gainst Carriacou champions. If we win, we go to Trinidad."

All the players started talking at once but Natty hammered on the table and shouted for silence again. "We playing a practice game on Saturday. The team up on the notice board. Let me know if you can play."

"Whatever the matter with Natty, man?" said Bashy. "He got a face long as a papaw."

The players milled round the notice board to see who had been picked for the practice game.

Little Riccardo had no chance of seeing over the crowd but Bashy stood on tip-toe.

"Game against *Siva Sugar*," he announced. "And I playing."

"Big surprise," said Riccardo sarcastically.

"Yes. You in the team too, Riccardo."

Riccardo's heart thumped. Bashy and Natty and Leo were great cricketers. But he'd show them. And *Calypso* would win and he'd play in the Valentine Shield, too... in Trinidad.

Chapter 2

Count Crawfish gave Jessie a piece of roti with goat curry. Jessie was Riccardo's dog, though Riccardo was never quite sure if she understood that. The only time she showed any signs of obeying him was when he was feeding her. Jessie worshipped food. It was the reason why she dived into all the village dustbins every morning and stood for hours outside the roti shop. And it was why she met Riccardo every evening after school at the Oval Ground where she knew that old Crawfish always had something delicious for her in his lunchbox. Goat curry was her favourite – she had a passion for spicy food.

"They telling me *Calypso* got a match tomorrow, Rikki Tikki," the Count said, as they settled down on their favourite bench by the boundary.

Rikki Tikki was one of the old poet's many nick-names for Riccardo – it came from Rikki Tikki Tavi, the mongoose in the famous story.

"Yeah. We got practice game. I playing," said Riccardo, trying not to show his delight too much.

"What you practising for?"

"We playing Valentine Shield match next week."

"Ah yes. Here at Oval ground, right?"

Riccardo nodded. The Count gave Jessie a second piece of roti and looked hard at Riccardo. Then he said slowly, "Pity you can't play that one, too."

"What you say?"

"You can't play cricket on Calypso Final Day. Can't be in two places in one go, man."

Riccardo felt a sudden sick lurch in his stomach. The Count was right. The Calypso Final… it was on the same day as the big match. Why hadn't he thought of that?

"I gotta play," he said fiercely.

"How?"

"Final can wait another year."

"Riccardo, think hard. Your name in the programme. On all the posters. What people say about you if you don't sing?"

Riccardo's brain searched wildly for an answer. How could he miss the game? The biggest game in *Calypso*'s history. It wasn't fair. "And if *Calypso* playing, I don't have no band," he said, as the full misery began to dawn on him. The band always followed the team on match days. How could he sing without them?

"Don't need a band, Rikki Tikki. Your sweet voice all you need."

"Don't have no song neither," said Riccardo.

"No song?"

"I can't write calypso no more. Can't find the words, can't find no tune."

"Easy, man. Those calypsos soon make a show. Don't fear."

"That's fine for you to say. You not in my calypso-writing shoes."

Count Crawfish smiled. "Those songs in your body and in your head, Rikki Tikki. You can't stop them coming out." He cleared his throat. "Show them what you got; sing the words on the spot. Improvise. Yes, man, calypso can be impro too. Listen to me."

Don't have no band, don't have no song.
Words when they coming, they coming wrong.

No more ideas coming my way;
Inspiration gone on holiday.

I biting my pen and staring at the clock
I only hearing the tick and the tock
I must be suffering from calypso block.

I look for ideas from Island politics;
I turn to the bedroom for little lyrics.
But neither sex scandal or social rage
Helping Crawfish to improve the blank page.

I biting my pen and staring at the clock
I only hearing the tick and the tock
I must be suffering from calypso block.

Riccardo loved to hear Crawfish sing; playing with words and rhythms like all the great calypso artists. But today his mind kept drifting away. He saw himself all alone on the stage at Constantine Bay. A sea of faces waiting for him to perform. Walking up to the microphone and opening his mouth to sing. And not a note coming out.

◦ ◦ ◦

Things started going badly wrong for *Calypso* even before the game with *Siva Sugar* CC. At net practice Desmond sprained his ankle. He was playing football, running to meet a cross, when he stepped on a cricket ball and went down writhing in pain. A lump the size of a sweet lime bulged out on the side of his ankle and he had to be carried back to the changing room. It didn't take a doctor to tell that he was out of the game. Ravi and Mylo pulled out too. Ravi had to go to his brother's wedding and Mylo had been off school sick all week with 'flu, which was a surprise to no one because it was exam week.

Riccardo, too, had offered to withdraw from the team. "What the point in practice if I don't play in the *Grand Bay* game?" he said to Natty.

"If you don't play, where I going to find another player?" Natty snapped back sharply and Riccardo left it at that.

The last straw came on the night before the fixture. There was a fire at the *Calypso* cricket pavilion. It would have burned to the ground but for a torrential rainstorm which put out the flames long before the fire engine arrived. The damage was bad enough, though – there a hole in the roof and the visitors' changing room was

flooded out. Worse still, three people had been seen running away from the ground just before the fire took hold and the police had been called in to investigate.

On the day of the match *Calypso*'s ground was strangely silent. The band had a booking at the hotel; they said they'd be along at tea-time. It was the first time that anyone could remember starting a game without the beat of the team's famous 'Bat and Ball' calypso anthem. It wasn't a good omen.

When the game finally got under way, it seemed as if everyone in the team had forgotten how to play cricket. Natty started it – dropping the easiest of catches in the slips. Then the rot really set in. In quick succession, Leo, Rohan and Ryan also put down simple chances. Leo was bowling fast as the wind but he sent down six wides in one over, so Natty had to take him off. And Bashy, of all people, fumbled a throw-in and missed a straight-forward run-out. Five chances went down in as many overs: the *Siva Sugar* openers were almost dancing for joy at their good fortune. The score-board skipped along – 40 ... 50 ... 60 for no wicket.

Riccardo, who, for once, hadn't yet tripped over his toes or let a ball go through his legs for four, watched in despair from the boundary. The sun burned down relentlessly on his maroon sun hat. Despair gave way to anger as he noticed three figures walking round the ground towards him. It was Snapper and his two shadows, Brainless Brian and K-man the Clown. Snapper was trouble, big trouble. Mean and wiry, with a permanent sneer on his lips, he gave Riccardo the creeps.

Riccardo stood and waited for the inevitable insults.

"Butter-Finger, man, give us catching class," said K-man.

"Care what you say, K-man," sneered Snapper. "Small-boy here a big hero now. He sing his way to fame."

Riccardo ignored the taunts. He kept his eyes fixed firmly on the cricket action but he sensed them still standing behind him right by the boundary rope, waiting their moment. They didn't have long to wait. The ball was hammered in Riccardo's direction. He ran in to field it, tripped over his feet and stumbled. Cackles of laughter rose behind him. He picked up the ball and bowled it underarm towards Bashy but only succeeded in throwing it straight up in the air. The laughter redoubled. He retrieved the ball and threw it in angrily. The batters had scampered an extra run.

Riccardo turned and walked back to the boundary and his three tormentors.

Snapper applauded ironically. "You born entertainer, Small-boy. Big future for you in the circus."

Riccardo turned his back on him.

"Little Butter-Finger here going to Calypso War," continued Snapper. "He think he beat Growling Pantha and Diabolo. But I tell him, take Snapper's advice. Watch his step or he fall flat on his face."

Again Riccardo said nothing and concentrated on watching Natty. He wasn't bowling well. And he wasn't showing much interest in his fielders either. Something was wrong with their captain, Riccardo was certain of it.

"And what this I see?" said Snapper in exaggerated surprise. "Hole in pavilion roof. Oh heavens! There been a fire, Small-boy?"

Brian sniggered. "Some clumsy fool knock over the kerosene can."

Snapper laughed. "Butter-Finger drop a lighted match and… *whoosh*."

Riccardo spun round angrily. "You know so much, Snapper, I wondering if you there last night and…"

"You want lick-up, Small-boy? You accusing me?"

Riccardo said nothing.

"Right answer, Butter-Finger. Best you keep your big mouth shut."

"Hey, look, man, ball coming your way," shouted Brian. Riccardo swung round. But the ball was nowhere near; it was in Bashy's hands. The trio laughed again.

"Me mistake. Chutney boy has it," said Brian.

Natty at long last woke up to Riccardo's plight and posted him to another fielding position, out of the reach of the three bullies. "See you soon, Butter-Finger," said Snapper. "See you at Calypso Final."

The jokers waved and moved on to seek out another victim.

Chapter 3

The carnage continued through the hot afternoon. Natty didn't seem to have a single idea in his head about how to stop the run riot. He brought back Leo, *Calypso*'s fastest bowler. And the faster he bowled the harder the batters slapped him over the ropes, pulling and cutting. Another six was smashed over mid wicket; a four through the covers. By the time the *Siva Sugar* opener tried one biff too many, the damage had been well and truly done.

The fielding side limped in to tea with a Himalayan mountain to climb: 230 to win. They had taken only four of the opposition's wickets and dropped three times as many catches.

"Never seen us play like that, man," Bashy said to Riccardo. "Everyone in the team to blame."

Riccardo munched a patty thoughtfully. What

worried him most was not the dropped catches or the wild bowling, but Natty. He'd let things drift and hadn't seemed to care. Natty had never been so quiet on a cricket field. "Better to have a bad game now. Get it off our chest before we play *Grand Bay*," he said to Bashy. And then he remembered he wouldn't be playing in the big game and his heart sank even further.

"Not over yet," said the ever-optimistic Bashy. "We a strong batting side. Natty get us off to a good start, then we chip away at they total, you see. If they can hit 229, we go one better."

None of the *Calypso* players had much of an appetite for tea. Even Rohan, who usually ate like two horses, had gone off his food. Natty was silent and sat on his own, head in hands. The arrival of Wesley and the band did little to revive the team's spirits. They played 'Bat and Ball' and a few of the team sang along half-heartedly:

> Today Bat and Ball will meet
> In a sweet calypso beat.
>
> Batsman, beat the shine,
> Bowler, find your line.

When the band begin to play
Bat and Ball will break away.

The umpires were already out in the middle; the tea break was over. Natty and Ritchie opened the batting – Ritchie standing in for Desmond, *Calypso*'s regular opener.

Four balls later, *Calypso* were 0 for three and the *Siva* fast bowler was dancing for joy, celebrating his hat trick: Natty clean-bowled second ball; Rohan given out *lbw* playing back and Chandra losing his middle stump to a quick yorker. After that it was just a matter of time. Bashy put up some fine resistance but wickets fell regularly at the other end. At 64 for eight, with the match long lost, Riccardo walked out to the middle.

"Time to enjoy ourselves. Beat the ball, man. Put some ginger in your shot," said Bashy, grinning confidently. Riccardo looked around... plenty of room to score runs, he thought. *Siva Sugar*'s attacking field meant that he only had to push the ball past all the players breathing down his neck.

Bashy battled on majestically. His half-century, one of the best Riccardo had ever seen him play, came in just 45 balls. Bashy was true class. He made batting look so simple. He waited motionless – waited for the ball to leave the bowler's hand – waited for it to bounce off the pitch and somehow he was in the right place to wait just long enough for it to hit the middle of his flowing bat. Riccardo could never hope to bat like him. But after a lucky edge had streaked through the slips to the boundary, Riccardo drove the next for four right off the meat of the bat. It was a top-class shot, and he went down the wicket to meet Bashy and they punched their gloves together.

"Keep it going, man," said Bashy, smiling under the grille of his helmet. "You never know what can happen on a cricket field."

But any hope of the great escape vanished next over. Bashy hit too early across a short ball and hoisted it straight up in the air. The keeper ran back to take a good catch, diving full length. Bashy swung his bat over his shoulder and walked off to generous applause.

In came number 11 – Leo.

Everyone knows Leo is the worst batter on the Island... probably the worst in the whole cricketing universe. He always closes his eyes as the bowler runs in. Bashy once said that since he can't see the ball, he must use his big ears as radar receivers.

Riccardo managed to keep the strike for nearly two overs but finally it was Leo's turn to square up to the bowling, and sadly for him the opening quick bowler was back. He speared a fast yorker into the tail-ender's toes. Leo didn't move and the ball struck him smack on the top of his left foot. As he hopped about, the whole *Siva* team screamed for *lb*w. The umpire didn't hesitate. "Out!" he shouted, and took off the bails for the end of the match.

Calypso were all out for 97. Riccardo was 15 not out. It was his highest score for the team. The *Siva* players swarmed round their fast bowler, who had taken seven wickets, and Riccardo set off, head down, for the pavilion. But then he spotted Leo, sitting on the ground, taking off his boot.

"Me toe broken, Small-boy," he whined. "I certain of it." He pulled of his sock to inspect the injury. His big toe was swelling and turning dark purple before Riccardo's eyes. If it was broken, they both knew that Leo would miss the *Grand Bay* game. And without their main strike bowler, their chances of winning were close to zero.

Leo leaned heavily on little Riccardo and they slowly hobbled off in the direction of the pavilion, with Big Lug whimpering at every step. The so-called 'warm-up' game had left *Calypso CC* out cold.

Chapter 4

"So what name we goin' to give you, Ricky boy?" asked Martha.

"Name?" said Riccardo, without really listening. His older sister didn't normally take much interest in him. Her little brother was mostly a source of irritation or amusement for her. But the Calypso Final had changed all that.

"Calypso singer need calypso name, like The Mighty Sparrow or Lord Invader," said Martha.

Riccardo sighed. But Martha didn't give up easily. "Remember that teacher at school who sing calypso? Call himself Chalkdust – good name for teacher, eh?"

It was true enough, every calypso singer had a special name: The Growling Pantha, Diabolo... Count Crawfish even... Riccardo often wondered what Crawfish's real name was but he didn't like to ask.

"I say we call you Un-Mighty Sparrow," said Martha, giggling at her own joke.

"Very funny."

"What is it old Crawfish call you? Rikki Tikki Tavi?"

Riccardo said nothing. He didn't mind his friend calling him Rikki Tikki, but there was no way he wanted the whole Island thinking he was named after a mongoose.

"Got it," said Martha, slapping her thigh in triumph, the way their mother did. "Only one name for my little calypso brother. He Butter-Finger."

Riccardo almost smiled. There'd been a time when he'd hated being called Butter-Finger. He had been taunted with the name because of his dropped catches and fumbling fielding. But after the Island Cup Final Butter-Finger had become a proud nickname, forever part of that famous victory. Yes, Butter-Finger he would be.

"What Butter-Finger going to sing?" asked Martha. Typical, thought Riccardo. His sister had a perfect knack for lifting the lid on bubbling trouble. His long wait for song-writing inspiration was showing no signs of coming to an end. In fact it was getting worse, because Riccardo was beginning to panic.

"I still writing," he said cagily.

"You want to hurry, brother. Final here in no time."

Riccardo shrugged.

"Don't try nothing too serious, boy. Remember you up against Pantha and that QueeAnB. They know how to please a crowd."

The five contestants in the Calypso Final had now been officially announced. The Growling Pantha, Diabolo and Roti Boy were there as expected. But QueeAnB was the surprise selection – an even bigger surprise than Riccardo. There'd been a lot of grumbling amongst the old purists that she was more disco than calypso, but no one disputed that QueeAnB was good enough. She had a big, melodic sound and a big character to match.

The singers could choose any subject they liked, but as Martha said, it was the crowd-pleasers that usually won the contest. The most popular calypsos were the ones that made fun of local politicians or other well-known characters. They were sometimes very rude. The Growling Pantha, the current reigning Monarch, had made a name for himself with his rude songs, specially when he sang about the local politicians or Diabolo; but none of the Island calypsonians was ruder than QueeAnB.

"That QueeAnB famous all over for her sexy calypsos," said Martha, and to Riccardo's dismay she wiggled her bum from side to side and sang one of the singer's saucy songs:

> Boys, boys, better mind
> Your length and line
> When QueeAnB
> Swing her shine,
> 'Cause rain
> Won't stop play
> When QueeAn
> Break away.

"Don't you try nothing like that, mind," said Martha, wagging her finger. "You too young for sexy stuff, little brother."

Riccardo scowled. "I sing what I like," he said. "None your business." He made for the kitchen door.

"Where you going?"

"See Count Crawfish."

"You mind what you doing with old Crawfish. You know what they saying?"

"What?"

"That he write you songs for you."

Riccardo was aghast. "That a lie and you know it. Crawfish never do that," he cried.

"OK, keep you cool, man. But you tell him watch out. If that rumour catch fire, it spell trouble for you both."

Riccardo scowled at his sister and stormed out. Jessie got up, licked her lips and followed him.

◎ ◎ ◎

"You still worry about Calypso War, eh, Rikki Tikki?" Count Crawfish asked.

"No," lied Riccardo. His sister's warning had shaken him. How could anyone believe he'd stolen his songs from Crawfish?

"Maybe I mistaken. Maybe you *are* too young."

"Too young?"

"Perhaps better to wait for another year come round. Plenty time to be crowned Calypso Monarch."

"And if I don't sing, what they say? That all these stories about you and me are true?"

Count Crawfish raised an eyebrow. "So you hear the gossip, too." The old man eased himself into his seat as he did when he was about to tell a story or sing a song. He sucked his teeth and gazed across the pitch to the palm trees.

"Last year I am a judge in Calypso Final," he began. "There are five judges and all five vote for Pantha. He sing the best songs – simple as that. But that Diabolo boy stir up trouble and say that judging biased. Everyone tell you that his singing not good enough but still he bitter about it and he point the finger at me... say I start conspiracy against him. A year ago I tell myself: I finish with judging job for good and all. But still the rumours spreading. He dangerous, that Diabolo. He and his friends putting about more dirty stories and I damn sure he the one behind this name-calling."

"I ain't bothered what he call me. Butter-Finger write his own songs," said Riccardo defiantly.

"Butter-Finger?" The old singer chuckled. "Butter-Finger – I like that name. Now Butter-Finger join the hall of fame along with Mighty Sparrow and King Radio." And he sang:

Who never heard of the Mighty Sparrow
Don't live in the world of calypso,
And if you mean to keep the rhyme-o,
What about Shadow and King Radio?

It is not Count Crawfish intention
To offend any calypsonian;
Famous names too numerous to mention
So forgive me the sin of omission.

I choose to begin with Lord Beginner,
That don't mean I forget Attila;
I take off my hat to Lord Kitchener
But I greet Growler, Invader, Caresser.

Ladies too jamming their mark on the scene.
Hello, Calypso Rose and Singing Francine;
Roll up for Drupattie, the Chutney Queen,
Lord, where all these female voices been?

Crawfish would stop here or take you further
Back to Roaring Lion and Executer;
But today let me introduce the future,
Put your hands together for a newcomer –

None other than mighty little Butter-Finger!
The mike is yours. Now, boy, deliver.
None other than mighty little Butter-Finger!
The mike is yours. Now, boy, deliver!

Count Crawfish sang the last two lines over and over, slapping his hand on the bench to beat out the tune. When he stopped, he put an arm round Riccardo's shoulder. "These lies serious, Butter-Finger. Best we don't do anything to feed the fire. I will not see you again before Butter-Finger fight Calypso War."

Jessie let out a low growl. "Sorry, Jessie. That mean no rotis for you for three days," said the Count. He smiled at Riccardo, who was frowning deeply. "Don't worry, Rikki Tikki, you'll write those songs and you'll have the whole Island cheering Butter-Finger."

Riccardo got up to leave.

"Just one more thing," said Count Crawfish.

"Yes?"

"Get yourself a chorus."

"Chorus?"

"Backing singers. You don't need a full band. But two, three singers drive along the rhythm. Give the crowd someone else to look at, too."

"But I don't know anyone…"

"Ask your sister. Maybe she and her friends can help find you singing group."

Riccardo felt very alone as he walked home, shooing Jessie past her favourite dustbins. It was true the Count had helped him with his poetry. He'd learned a lot about rhythm and lyrics from the old calypsonian. Sometimes he'd borrowed a Crawfish line and changed the words or a picked up on a special beat, but he'd never stolen a thing. All Riccardo's songs were his own from beginning to end.

Now he had to prove it.

Chapter 5

Leo's big toe was broken in two places; he turned up at net practice with a crutch and his whole foot wrapped in a massive bandage. He had a set of x-rays that he showed proudly to anyone he could corner. Desmond, too, was still limping on his swollen ankle. His chances of playing in the game were no better than fifty-fifty.

But the injury news was overshadowed by another story. Natty had led *Calypso CC* for two years. He'd always been a popular captain and a good one, too – although sometimes he could be thoughtless and insensitive. But no one had ever seen him behaving like this before.

Bashy and Riccardo were watching Natty batting in the nets. He looked miserable. Even when he hit the ball off the meat of the bat there was no joy in his eyes. It was as if he was in a trance.

"He tell Rohan he the worst bowler ever seen in the Caribbean," said Bashy.

"You joking."

"Ain't no joke, man. Natty acting strange strange."

"What wrong with him?"

"Your guess as good as mine," said Bashy. "But something troubling him, that for sure. And *Calypso Cricket Club* suffering for it."

Riccardo nodded. The defeat against *Siva Sugar* hadn't been all Natty's fault by any means. Everyone had played badly. But there had been no leadership, no one in charge pulling things back together when they went wrong. *Calypso* was accustomed to having a strong captain – and he had gone missing.

"Someone need to talk to him," said Riccardo.

"Yeah," agreed Bashy. Riccardo stared at his friend long and hard and Bashy's eyes widened. "You not saying I do it, are you?" he said.

"Who else?"

Bashy scratched his head thoughtfully. "OK, I give it a try if I get a chance."

The chance came sooner than he expected. Rohan was fired up in the nets by what Natty had said and trying to bowl much too fast. Suddenly he unleashed a wicked beamer. It was a complete accident – the ball slipped out of his hand and it flew at Natty head-high. Natty ducked, but it struck him smack on the elbow.

For a moment he stood still, shaking a little. Then the pain piled in. He grasped his injured arm, turned and swore at Rohan and then, with amazing violence, he hurled his bat at him. The bowler, who had followed through halfway down the wicket, only just swerved out of the way in time. Rohan looked shocked at first, but then he laughed. For a moment, it looked as if Natty was going to throw a punch at him. But instead he stormed straight past Rohan out of the nets and ran towards the pavilion... and everyone could see that he was crying.

Training came to a halt. All the players stood around looking embarrassed.

"Didn't do it deliberate. Honest, man," insisted Rohan.

"Not your problem," said Ravi, staring after the departing captain.

Bashy glanced at Riccardo and set off after Natty.

The practice session resumed but it soon turned into a farce. No one was concentrating. The batters slogged and the bowlers bowled bouncer after bouncer, mostly way off target. Ravi got hit on the shoulder by a ball that was smashed out of the net and Mylo took a solid thump on the helmet from a bouncer. It was amazing that no one got seriously hurt.

After a while Bashy returned. "Natty going home," he told everyone as they gathered round.

"He must be sick," said Ravi.

"Don't think so," said Bashy. "Don't know what's wrong with him. He won't tell me nothing. But I got some news."

"What?"

"We need to choose a new captain."

There was a murmur of surprise from the players and a few shocked looks.

"Natty say he don't want to lead the team 'gainst *Grand Bay*. Say he can't do it."

"So what we going to do?" asked Rohan.

"Like I tell you. Choose a new captain."

Natty had been captain for as long as anyone could remember. No one seemed to have much idea how to set about picking a new one.

Desmond made a suggestion. "Nominations…

that's what we need," he said. "We got to nominate someone."

"I nominate Desmond," said Rohan.

"I can't be captain. I can't hardly walk," said Desmond firmly.

"Don't make no sense to pick a captain who don't play," agreed Ravi.

"If everyone says they not going to do it, we won't get nowhere," said Bashy.

"I nominate you," said Riccardo quietly.

"Me! You crazy?"

"Face it, man, you the only choice," said Ravi. "You the best player."

"Best player don't make the best captain," protested Bashy.

"Any other nominations?" asked Desmond. No one spoke. "Then Bashy captain for one game," he said firmly.

"Well, thanks, man," said Bashy sarcastically. "And what if we lose?"

"Then you the one we blame, of course," said Desmond.

Nets came to an end and the players packed away the kit, still talking about the sudden turn of events. Riccardo noticed a lonely figure walking away from the ground. Was Natty in some sort of trouble, he wondered? Or was he sick? He surely wouldn't give up being captain without a very good reason.

But soon Natty was forgotten. There were plenty of other things for the players to talk about. Carnival was on everyone's mind. And tomorrow was the first day of Carnival, when the Island would awake to the biggest party of the year.

Chapter 6

On the Island, Carnival arrives each year with the *boom boom* of the big drums and the drone of the conch shells. Soon the music takes over: kaiso, soca, bouyou – all the sounds of the jump-up. Next come the stick fights. Village champions gather together to do battle and the bands play and then the conch shell sounds for the first contest.

Bashy and Riccardo pushed to the front of the crowd to see the first two stick fighters emerge. Their drummers beat up a wild frenzy, louder and faster, faster and louder, the drumsticks becoming a blur as the drummers yelped and screamed, whipping up the crowd. Now they gave way to the batonniers... the famous stick fighters. A tall, skinny guy, bald head shining bright in the sun, rushed forward, holding his poui stick in front of his face. He sang his challenge to his drummer's beat, stamping his right foot down hard as he chanted:

Live according to greed
And you will eat the bread
That the Devil knead;
Red is the blood all-o'-we bleed,
So, partner, better mind your head.

Lick for lick and blow for blow
I wielding my poui stick
Quicker than batsman willow.
Who is not me friend, don't join de ring

My stick name Scorpion
And Scorpion got sting.

So, bring on the opposition
In the stick-fight competition,
For I am judge and jury
And long is the arm of my poui;
It will follow you down to hell
'Cause mercy is a word my stick can't spell.

His adversary rushed at him, long dreadlocks swinging wildly. He was shorter but much brawnier than the first fighter and he lashed out at the singer. One, two, three blows of his stick. The singer parried the blows in front of his head and struck back one-handed. Dreadlocks swung away and did a mocking dance, hair and sweat flying, but the bald batonnier caught him a blow on the arm in mid-dance. Then he too broke into a dance and the crowd joined in with the song.

Tell your mamma, band she belly and bawl
'Cause today, today she son bound to fall –
If you too weak to walk, you can always crawl...

More savage blows; it seemed certain bones would be broken. But the fighters were as skilled at dodging and parrying as they were at handing out the punishment. They danced and stamped and circled each other and the sticks clashed. And then, in the blink of an eye, one of the fighters fell in a cloud of dust. Dreadlocks lay on his back. The tall batonnier was the winner.

Dreadlocks shuffled away, hunched and beaten. Everyone swayed to the drumming as the victor celebrated his win with another hip-swinging dance.

"They faking it, man," hissed an old man in the crowd close to Bashy and Riccardo. "In the old days the fighters hard as pepper. You see blood flow every time."

"We should go look for Natty." Bashy nudged Riccardo, reminding him of why they were there. They had been out searching for Natty when they'd come across the stick fighters. Natty hadn't gone home after net practice. No one knew where he was. His family had been out hunting for him all night, and half the village, too. Riccardo and Bashy had scoured all his haunts: the cricket ground, the harbour, the beach, but there was no sign of him anywhere.

As new batonniers emerged to do battle, the two friends pushed their way out of the crowd and headed for the beach again.

"He gone to ground. That for sure," said Riccardo.

"Not easy to disappear on the Island. Always someone watching," said Bashy.

They walked along the palm tree coast where the young kids were swimming and playing noisy games of cricket. The two friends sat down on the sand and watched the waves from the Atlantic roll in.

"May have to call off the game," said Bashy.

"Why?"

"We only nine without Natty and Desmond. Can't play with nine players." Bashy wrote all the names down in the sand with his finger.

Mylo
Ritchie
Bashy
Ahir
Chandra
Ravi
Rohan
Ryan
Cuthbert

Natty
Desmond

"Who's Cuthbert?" asked Riccardo.

"Little brother of Ritchie. He only ten but Ritchie say he spin the ball square. Bowling not too bad: three spinners, and Rohan and Ryan bowling seam. But nobody with Leo's pace and bounce."

"Wish I playing," said Riccardo quietly.

"Me too," said Bashy. "You write those songs yet?"

Riccardo shook his head.

"Carnival bring you inspiration," said Bashy. "Look on the bright side. We'll have double celebration. You Calypso Monarch and *Calypso CC* bound for Trinidad." Bashy always looked on the bright side.

"Sure," said Riccardo, unconvinced. "I guess it turn out all right."

"Forget you troubles, man. Tonight time to relax," said Bashy. "7 o'clock. Don't be late." Bashy's family was holding a fete. Canboulay fetes were the big Carnival family feasts; they were held all over but none of them would be bigger than Bashy's. His family was one of the oldest Indian families on the Island, and one of the largest.

"You don't want to miss the food, man," said Bashy. "My mum the best cook in the Caribbean, you'll see."

◉ ◉ ◉

At twilight the guests started arriving at the fête in large numbers, though Bashy's brothers and sisters

and aunts and uncles and grandfathers and grandmothers easily outnumbered them. They'd come laden with patties and rotis. There were great bowls of mangoes and papaws and starapples and pineapple slices rubbed with salt and sugar too, and tarts and puddings – sugar cake and pine tarts and sweet rice and kulfi in beds of melting ice. In the middle of the yard Bashy's mother was roasting a goat over an open fire. Big pots of sweet potatoes and dhal and peas bubbled alongside it. The sweet aroma of cooking and smoke filled the air and the guests talked noisily in the flickering light of the fire.

Then more lights. A torch procession of revellers and musicians filed into the yard. They greeted the guests with shouts and the beat of the big drum and the low boom of the conch shells. Other musicians took up the rhythm. Riccardo, who had arrived just ahead of the torches, recognised the players of the Island's All Stars Band: the steel drum and the cornet and the bongo and the guitar struck up.

The beat quickened and the guests joined the revellers in a traditional Creole dance; the torches were swung and tossed in the air, throwing strange elongated shadows across the yard as the fire glowed and flickered.

Riccardo saw Bashy dancing with his sister and her two best friends, Millie and Janine. He quite liked Millie but Janine, the pretty one, was always teasing him… especially about how he kept falling over his feet. For once, though, he was half-pleased to see them: it was his chance to ask the question that was on his mind.

As the revellers piled their plates high with mounds of goat roti and rice, the musicians sat and played. It was then that Riccardo saw Crawfish sitting amongst them. He was laughing and beckoning to Bashy's grandfather to come and join them with his tassa drum.

Finally persuaded, the old man shuffled over and sat down cross-legged, the clay drum in his lap. With all eyes on him, he coaxed out a strange haunting sound from the drum skin with the long wooden beaters, and the band clapped out a rhythm. The Count sat down beside the old drummer and they sang together.

When I was a boy I learn this recipe
Straight from the mouth of my aunty Drupattie.
She say, listen and listen carefully
To how you make this music they call chutney.

Stir up de tempo
In de tassa,
Spice up de lingo
With masala.

Blend sweet calypso
With a curry flavour,
Boy, let it simmer
In de rhythm fire.

You don't have to be a Trinie
To learn this chutney recipe,
But I have to say I am very glad
I got it straight from my aunty in Trinidad.

She even teach me a few words of Hindi;
So I can call me grandfather Daa-Daa-Jee,
And if you see Daa-Daa-Jee dance de chutney!
Man, if you see Daa-Daa-Jee winey-winey! ...

Then the revellers and the band were gone in a
trail of torchlight and music and the guests and
family settled down to eat. Riccardo, who hadn't
spoken a word to Count Crawfish, filled his plate
with goat curry and peas and joined Bashy and the
three girls.

"Butter-Finger here to sing us a calypso," said Millie, seeing Riccardo pushing through the crowd towards them.

"Oh please, please, let us hear what you sing at the Final, Rikki boy," said Janine.

Riccardo shook his head. "It a secret…"

"Always a secret! What we have to do to persuade Butter-Finger?" Janine giggled, and then snorted with laughter as Riccardo dropped his fork in embarrassment.

"I looking for a backing group," Riccardo blurted out crossly.

"Backing group?" said Martha.

"You know… to sing with me."

"Up there on stage at Constantine Bay with you, Rikki boy?" said Janine. She'd stopped laughing.

"You want harmony singers to accompany you?" said Millie. Riccardo nodded. The three girls looked at each other and slapped their hands together.

"Ready for audition, Calypso Boy?" said Janine.

"What?"

"We gon sing to you," said Martha.

And before Riccardo could utter another word,

the girls linked arms and launched into their version of a song everyone knows.

> Yellow bird, up high on banana tree,
> Yellow bird, how you like this melody?
> Butter-Finger wants tree singing friend
> So hear our tree voices blend.
> And we won't fly away, in the sky away
> On calypso final day.
> No, we'll be there to accompany
> Butter-Finger the Un-mighty.

They took a bow at the end and Bashy clapped. "Don't need to look no further, man," he said to

Riccardo. "They make a sweet sound."

"We hired?" asked Millie, jumping up and down in excitement.

"Er, well..." said Riccardo – he knew he was losing control of things.

"We don't let you down, Riccardo," said Janine, giving him a big kiss.

"When's the rehearsal?" asked Martha.

"Only one day to go before Final," said Millie.

"Tomorrow morning at our house," said Martha. Riccardo nodded feebly. The girls were taking him under their wing. But whatever would they say, he wondered, when he told them he hadn't written a single song?

◦ ◦ ◦

The party went on until the early hours. Riccardo forgot his troubles and joined in the jump-up. He even danced with Janine and he didn't tread on her toes once.

But later that evening, as the guests began to leave, he sat alone in a corner of the yard. Bashy's grandfather was still tapping out a gentle rhythm on the tassa and Riccardo's thoughts drifted off to his friend, Bashy and the team.

A few lines floated into his head.

> Heaven is a place I never been
> But they tell me is a glorious green;
> That is why I come to the conclusion
> Heaven is a cricket ground.

Soon he was scribbling in his red book. Line after line, the song poured out. When he'd finished, he sang it under his breath. There was no doubt, it was a calypso. A real live calypso at last!

Chapter 7

By the morning of the Calypso Final, Carnival was in full swing. All over the Island could be heard the booming of drums and the lilting ping-pong rhythm of the steel bands. The big steel pan bands on their flat-bed motor trucks led the revellers through the streets. Like the surge of the sea, the rhythms slowed and quickened as the drummers swayed and sweated in their glittery costumes. Around the bands swarmed the masqueraders, leaping and wining up through the streets. Sometimes a drummer would jump down into the crowd, playing on the run, flinging himself about wildly to the swirl of the beat.

All the traditional characters of the mas mingled with even stranger, home-made costumes: men in grass skirts and painted faces and big feather head-dresses and women disguised as pirates and sailors. A large woman wearing a Pope's gown and mitre was singing from a Bible which she held upside down; another was dressed as a tropical Osama bin Laden with a long beard and turban

and a short sequined skirt. There were Bushes and Blairs in bikinis and bearded men in baby costumes and glittery gowns stretched over big wire frames and girls in top hats and Indian head dresses – all laughing and reeling and shouting and chanting.

Then came the sensay mas players, shaggy in their head-to-toe rope and black satin outfits, looming towards the children and leering through grotesque masks, shaking their massive horns and stamping their big boots studded with bottle tops noisily on the hard surface of the road. The children screamed and the dancers swayed on, clacking their feet.

As Riccardo walked slowly towards Constantine Bay the bands and their revellers passed, one by one. The Final was still two, maybe three hours away but he wanted to be there early.

A creature with devil's horns and raggedy clothes leapt out of the crowd towards him. It was Djab djab – a single monster formed by two men chained together and smeared with charcoal. All the children feared Djab djab. At carnival time he roamed the streets scaring them with his grimaces and gibberish. As a small boy Riccardo had been terrified of him, and he instinctively backed away when the limping, four-legged creature lurched into his path,

"The chains! Help bury Mama!" Djab djab shrieked, pulling a hideous face and beating on a biscuit tin. "Mother of Grace! Mother, mother, mother!" And in a cracked voice he half-sang and half-chanted:

> I am Djab djab
> The one with the horn,
> I throw me fowl
> To catch me corn.
>
> Nonsense is my modda,
> Gibberish my fadda,
> I look backward to my future
> And forward to my past.
>
> I sleep on a bed of ashes
> And bathe my skin in molasses.
>
> For I am Djab djab
> And I come out to play mas
> Among the masses.
>
> Djab djab dead but still alive

In this carnival jump and jive.

Holy Mother of Grace,
Look down with pity
On this human race.

With a cackle of laughter Djab djab limped on.
Riccardo jumped, as he heard another evil laugh
behind him. "Scared of Djab djab, Small-boy?
Time you stop being a big baby if you old enough
to sing in Final." It was Snapper, flanked as usual by
K-man and Brian. In their big feather headdresses
and grass skirts they looked more ridiculous than
sinister, but Riccardo was immediately on his guard.

Led by Snapper, the three did a mocking dance
in a circle around Riccardo, pulling faces and
laughing scornfully.

"Great calypso singer, gimme you autograph, man," jeered K-man.

"Mighty Butter-Finger, what song you sing for us today?" said Brian "Sing it me now."

"Whatever he sing he come last, certain sure," hissed Snapper, who had stopped dancing and now stood toe-to-toe with Riccardo. He pressed his face up close and stared at Riccardo with his cold eyes.

"Two defeats coming your way, Small-boy," he snarled. "Butter-Finger get last in the Final and *Calypso Cricket Club* get licks from Carriacou boys."

Riccardo walked on, but Snapper grabbed his shoulder. "*Calypso* get big licks with chutney-boy captain."

Riccardo pulled away angrily. "Bashy best cricketer on the Island," he said.

"Chutneys go play in chutney team," sneered Snapper. "Why you make chutney-boy captain, eh?"

"I ain't listening to no name-calling," said Riccardo defiantly.

"You want to hear what names chutneys call me?" snarled Snapper. "I say why you make Indian boy captain of *Calypso CC*?"

"Because..." began Riccardo.

"Because real captain run off like he a teef and hide hisself. *Calypso CC* bringing disgrace to the Island."

"Natty no teef," said Riccardo angrily. "You don't know nothing, Snapper."

"Don't excite youself, Small-boy. Make that voice of yours go all out of tune." Snapper gave Riccardo a poke in the chest and a sly grin. "Snapper know plenty thing you don't. You can dream of being big star, but remember ... Diabolo win Calypso War. Big trouble if he don't."

He wheeled away to join the other dancers with K-man and Brian, jeering and pointing back at Riccardo as they disappeared into the crowd.

Another band rolled past with a group of stilt dancers towering above the flat-bed truck. It was the All Stars Band. Riccardo recognised the voice of the band's singer before he caught sight of him. Crawfish was singing a brand new song he'd written specially for Carnival, and the crowd loved it. They were chanting the words and clapping to the beat.

> Carnival
> Is time
> To play any role.

Carnival
Is time
Shy does turn bold.

Man wearing woman petticoat,
Woman with beard down past her throat;
Who behind the mask you never know,
A mopsie Rosie could be a Rambo.

Carnival
Is time
To lose identity.
Carnival
Is time
For mask and be merry.

Today the poor man will wear a crown,
The bad John prancing in the judge's gown
Reversing roles in the revelry;
The mighty will be little and the little mighty
Reversing roles in the revelry;
A He will turn a She and a She turn a He.

The old poet spotted Riccardo in the crowd as the truck went past and he waved. "Good luck, Rikki Tikki," he shouted in the middle of his song.

The procession rolled on towards Constantine Bay and the sweet sound of the pans faded into the distance. Riccardo was left alone with his wandering thoughts.

He thought of Natty. What was he doing now? Where was he hiding? His mind then drifted on to Bashy and *Calypso CC*, taking him to the Oval ground and on to Trinidad, the big island over the sea where he'd never been, but Uncle Alvin had told him plenty about it. Brian Lara came from Trinidad, and many other West Indian greats.

Now, thinking about Snapper and his mates, Riccardo was tugged back to Constantine Bay. They would be there shouting for Diabolo. He frowned at the thought of what Snapper had said about Bashy, smiled as he remembered Count Crawfish's song, then frowned again as he wondered what Martha Millie and Janine would say when he told them he only had one song to sing.

The Calypso Final had sent the three girls into a frenzy. They were forever talking about their performance and what they were going to wear, practising their dance steps and telling Riccardo where he had to stand on stage. He was beginning to think he'd made a big mistake... until he saw them in action. Their batting and bowling dance routine for his new calypso, 'Heaven is a cricket ground', was as good as any professional group. And they sang like angels. Riccardo had never realised his sister had such a good voice. The girls loved the new song but, of course, as soon as they'd rehearsed it a few times, they wanted to know about the second one. Where was it – the big crowd-pleaser? Why didn't they have another song to rehearse?

"It a surprise," Riccardo insisted. But they wouldn't let him off the hook that easily.

"When we going to practise it?" Millie asked.

"What you song about?" Martha demanded.

"Why you keeping us in the dark, little Rikki?" Janine pleaded.

What could he say? It would be a surprise, all right, for everyone at Constantine Bay when he stood up on stage with nothing to sing. They'd be disgraced, booed off, ridiculed. And he couldn't let that happen to Martha and her friends.

Even now his thoughts returned to Natty. Was he hurt? Lying injured somewhere? Or had he turned up at the Oval at the last moment to play for *Calypso*? How Riccardo wished he was there now instead of facing this ordeal.

Snapper's words rang in his head again – "Chutneys go play in chutney team" – and his face burned hot with anger. The Island was made up of people from all over the world: African, European, Chinese and East Indians – or 'chutneys', as Snapper called them. Everyone used the word – there was chutney music and chutney food – it wasn't insulting. Yet somehow it was the way Snapper said it.

To stop his thoughts racing away, Riccardo opened up his song book and sat down by the side of the road and wrote:

> Carnival
> Is time
> For every waist to wine;
> Carnival
> Is time
> For every race to shine.

He sang the words under his breath. It was a good song, but he knew exactly where it had come from... he'd picked up the rhythm and even the words from the calypso he'd just heard Count Crawfish sing. If he sang it on stage, it was bound to stir up all that nonsense again about Crawfish writing his material for him. But the tune had got him started, got the juices flowing. And within moments he was scribbling in his book once more.

⊙ ⊙ ⊙

There was a crowd of maybe a hundred at the Oval when Bashy arrived. They were mostly gathered in the Ramadhin stand and in the shade under the palm trees.

Desmond was quite determined to play, even though he was still limping. Without Natty they'd have only ten players, including young Cuthbert. But with ten they could play the game ... even though it was a big handicap.

The *Grand Bay* players were already out practising on the out-field in front of the pavilion. They looked fit and athletic. One of the team, a tall, broad-shouldered boy, was bowling fast at a single stump. Bashy watched him send down five balls;

three times the stump cartwheeled out of the ground. Finally, having seen enough, he walked up and introduced himself as *Calypso*'s captain.

The tall boy took Bashy's hand. "I'm Julian," he said. "Captain of *Grand Bay*. Nice ground, man."

"You want to toss straight away?" said Bashy.

"Fine."

If you win the toss, think about it... and then bat. That's what Count Crawfish said you must always do at the Oval. Julian called heads. The coin landed... it was tails.

"We'll bat," said Bashy. Natty can go in down the order if he arrives late, he thought optimistically.

"Hot day," said Julian. "Good toss to win."

And he strolled over to his team to tell them that they were in the field.

Bashy wasn't sure about opening the batting with the injured Desmond. But what else could he do? Desmond and Ritchie at one and two... followed by Chandra and Ahir and then himself at five. After that he'd have to think – depending on how many runs there were on the board. But whatever the order, it was a long, long tail.

Chapter 8

Constantine Bay had drawn the whole Island to it like a magnet. The sea lapped at the edge of the vast crowd that filled the beach and spilled over on to the rocks, which looked like the terraces of a football stadium on a local cup derby day. The Calypso Final – or Calypso Tent, as some of the older Islanders called it – was the biggest and the best party of Carnival. The music of a pan band, playing on the little wooden stage above the beach, was all but drowned out by the crescendo of noise coming from the chanting fans.

The Growling Pantha's supporters had taken up

their pitch in the middle of the beach. There were hundreds of them singing over and over again the victory calypso that had won last year's Final. Diabolo's camp further to the left tried in vain to drown them out by chanting and waving pictures of their own hero. Some stilt dancers swayed to and fro with a huge Diabolo banner: 'Calypso Justice for Diabolo', it said – and everyone knew what it meant.

Towards the rocks, a big faction of Roti Boy's fans were dancing and leaping. The women and quite a lot of the men, too, were wearing bright-coloured saris – and many of them had painted their faces, arms and chests bright blue.

"Riccardo Small?" said a quiet voice in his ear. Riccardo jumped. He had been standing gazing in awe at the huge crowd from the shade of the stage. As he turned to reply, he trod on the foot of a short, plump, round-faced woman and nearly knocked her flying.

"S–sorry," he said.

"No harm done," said the woman, crossly retrieving her clipboard which had been knocked to the ground. A badge on her red T-shirt said 'Official'. "You'll be singing at number three in the first round," she snapped.

"Oh," said Riccardo, as calmly as he could.

"Pantha first. Then Roti Boy, Butter-Finger, QueeAnB and Diabolo," she said, glancing down at the clip board. "You have a backing group, I see."

Right on cue there was a chant from the crowd, "*Butter-Finger. BUTTER-FINGER.*" And, pushing through the throng towards them, came Martha, Millie and Janine.

"You not believe it, brother – everybody here from school," said Martha, giving Riccardo a big embarrassing hug.

"Plenty support behind you, Rikki boy," said Janine. "You near as many fans as Growling Pantha."

"This me backing group," said Riccardo shyly to the woman official, who nodded and wrote down the three girls' names on her pad as they practised the *Heaven is a cricket ground* routine by the edge of the stage. To Riccardo's amazement they didn't appear to be the slightest bit nervous.

The crowd was getting restless. Riccardo was about to tell the girls about the second song when a man in a shiny black suit appeared on stage and tried to speak into the microphone. He was drowned out by booing and foot-stamping. Finally he gave up and angrily stomped off to the biggest cheer of the day so far.

At last the pans were cleared from the stage and an eerie silence fell across the bay.

Then Pantha appeared. He walked on wearing white overalls and a big white space-man's helmet. As he turned away from the audience the word MONARCH was revealed, printed on his back; cheers and whistles rang through the crowd with a few loud boos from the Diabolo section.

At that moment Ricardo caught sight of Snapper and his two bodyguards – they were leading the booing. Snapper was shaking a fist aggressively at the figure on stage.

Everywhere is war and confusion
Growling Pantha might have the solution.
The United Nations trying, but things looking bad,
So is time they seek advice from Trinidad.
Now the Pantha has pondered global affairs,

And to me the answer is simple and clear:
I say, send the human race to Mars atmosphere
And leave the animals to take over down here.

Pantha's song, 'Destination Mars' was delivered to a catchy soca rhythm in the fine, strong voice everyone knew so well. It began slow like a missile lifting off, fighting the Earth's gravity.

I say, send them humans far –
Destination Mars, if you want to stop wars.
Destination Mars, I hear, is a nice place.
Leave Planet Earth to the four-foot race.

The crowd rose as one to the political message in the song, and the excitement grew with the speeding up of the tempo.

So, if you want peace and contentment
Across every nation and continent,
How about a turtle for a president?
I say, it would make more common sense
To have a donkey for minister of defence,
Yes, is time we hand over foreign policy
To a pussy-cat or a chimpanzee;
No, this human world order is not for me.

Destination Mars – I say, send them humans far,
Destination Mars, if you want to stop wars.
Destination Mars, I hear, is a nice place.
Leave planet earth to the four-foot race.

As Pantha sang the final bars a curtain behind him was drawn back ... and there stood a shiny silver rocket. Down its length in huge letters were the words MONARCH GROWLING PANTHA. With a roll of drums and plumes of red smoke, it lifted off from the stage. The smoke engulfed Pantha and in an instant he was gone. The audience stamped and screamed for more.

As the red smoke billowed across the bay, Riccardo wondered how he could begin to compete with such a polished performance. He felt sorry for Roti Boy, too, who had to follow the Monarch. After a short break while the rocket was removed, Roti Boy appeared in a pair of dazzling gold-sequined trousers. His bare chest and face were painted bright blue, just like his fans. He bowed and launched straight into a catchy chutney soca tune entitled, 'Paint the town blue, Lord Krishna'.

Riccardo didn't understand all the words but the rhythm was catchy. He was still tapping his feet to the beat long after the song ended. Then his heart leapt as the applause died down. Everyone was looking his way. It was his turn. He was on.

He stood up shakily and looked around for Martha and Co. but they were nowhere to be seen.

Butter-Finger, Butter-Finger, chanted his school friends. Riccardo edged forward nervously from the back of the stage. There was a gasp when he stumbled into the microphone and a roar of laughter as the stand went flying into the crowd. Some technicians rushed on to repair the damage and Riccardo stood watching them in horror, praying that a trap door would open in the floor and swallow him up. He had never felt so alone.

There was another burst of applause and a few whistles and Riccardo turned to see Martha, Millie and Janine at the back of the stage, dressed in the West Indies maroon cricket colours, pads and helmets ... and enormous polystyrene hands as big as tennis racquets. The girls attempted to throw a massive, bouncy red cricket ball back and forth to each other. It was hard to catch with their unwieldy hands and each time they dropped it, the crowd cried 'Butter-Finger!'

Riccardo froze ... but Martha winked at him and all three started humming *Heaven is a cricket*

ground into their microphones and waving at him to sing. The crowd picked up on it and gave Riccardo an encouraging round of applause. He took hold of the mike, stepped carefully over the lead and moved to the very front of the stage.

Heaven is a place I never been,
But they tell me is a glorious green;
That is why I come to the conclusion
Heaven is a cricket ground.
So, when the Day of Judgment come
I ain't waiting for no trumpet to blow,
I listening for the leather and the willow,
'Cause Butter-Finger say heaven is a cricket ground,
Yes, heaven is a cricket ground.

Bowler appeal,
Hand in the air,
Like he saying a prayer,
Like he really believe:
Ask, and you shall receive.

Batsman raise
He bat to the skies
Like he reach paradise,
Like he giving God the praise

Is another ton of runs!
I talking cricket, but it sound like religion,
And bat and ball too seeking salvation;
I don't know the saint from the sinner
But the umpire finger is the judgment finger
And only rain is the holy saviour.
Yes, when the Day of Judgment come
I ain't waiting for no trumpet to blow,
I listening for the leather and the willow,
'Cause Butter-Finger say heaven is a cricket ground,
Yes, heaven is a cricket ground.

He took his bow and the audience erupted. They clapped and whistled longer and louder than they had even for Pantha. Riccardo and his singers were called back on stage three times by the cheering, foot-stamping fans.

As he took his final bow, looking down at the sea of smiling faces below the stage, he met someone's eye. It was Natty, waving up at him.

As Riccardo stared, Natty gave him a double thumbs-up sign and then he was gone, melting back into the crowd so quickly that Riccardo wondered whether he had been seeing things.

Chapter 9

Just as Riccardo took his final bow, Bashy was walking out to the wicket. Things were not going well at the Oval. Bashy looked at the scoreboard: 27 for three. He was already regretting his decision to bat. Desmond got a bad *lbw* decision and he was still moaning about it in the changing room; the other two had been clean bowled. *Grand Bay's* fast opening attack had *Calypso* on the back foot, ducking and hopping about.

Ahir wasn't looking confident. He walked slowly towards the advancing Bashy.

"You leaving the ball well today," said Bashy with a grin. Ahir had played and missed so many times that the *Grand Bay* players had almost run out of 'oohs' and 'ahs'.

Ahir smiled sheepishly. "Ball leaving me," he said. "It moving about all over. Can't get me bat on it."

Bashy took guard, faced his first delivery ... and missed. Get forward, he told himself. It made no difference. The next ball swung away from him and the wicketkeeper gave a groan of disappointment as it thudded into his gloves.

"Catching practice coming soon," he said, as he threw the ball to the slip fielder alongside him. "This joker ain't lasting long."

The catching practice came at the other end. Ahir at last made contact with the ball and steered an edge straight into slip's hands. Chandra went first ball, caught and bowled. 27 for five. The *Calypso* supporters fell completely silent and the only sound in the ground came from the *Grand Bay* players clapping each other and cheering on their bowlers.

Game over before tea, if we don't do something quick, thought Bashy.

He got off the mark with a cover drive. It wasn't right off the middle of the bat but it flew across the hard outfield all the way to the boundary.

That feels better, he thought, and walked down the pitch for a quiet word with Ravi, the new batter.

Those who saw Bashy bat that day will always tell you about the majestic way he hit the ball, whipping it away wristily, playing the gaps in the field. But his performance wasn't just about his own batting. He encouraged and coaxed the tail enders, busily talking to them at the end of every over, keeping their concentration going through the afternoon heat.

It was like batting in a pressure cooker. Under the furnace of the sun the bowling was fast and accurate, the fielding aggressive and the sledging never let up. Ravi took a rising ball on the shoulder and turned away in pain, but without flinching.

"You dancing to me chin music, man?" shouted the bowler.

"Rub it. You know it hurt," said the wicket-keeper callously.

Bashy knew there was only one way to silence the opposition's taunts: deeds, not words were needed. He tried to hold on to the strike and keep the score moving, too. If the ball was a fraction short, he cut or pulled. If it was pitched up, he drove hard. One on-drive was timed so sweetly that the fielder on the boundary hardly moved a muscle before the ball flashed across the rope. But not even Bashy could stop wickets falling at the other end. Ravi fenced and battled. He was struck on the arm again before being caught in the slips off his glove – he and Bashy put on 21 runs. Rohan hung around for a time but a straight yorker finally saw him off. The score had reached 99 by the time the eighth wicket fell; Bashy was on 48.

As he watched little Cuthbert walking nervously out to bat, Bashy made up his mind. It was the last wicket stand... and they needed to make it count. *Calypso* would go down in a blaze of glory.

Cuthbert looked even smaller than he had in the changing room. His pads seemed enormous and he peered out from behind the grille of a massive red helmet. He had one ball of the over to face. Bashy could hardly bear to watch. But the young lad plonked his foot bravely down the wicket and played a perfect forward defensive shot. Bashy smiled and walked down the wicket to punch gloves.

Looking for the knock-out blow, Julian, *Grand Bay*'s captain, brought himself back on to bowl at the Ramadhin stand end. He'd already taken four wickets and he was after his 'fi'for'.

Crack. Bashy hit the first ball back over his head for four. The crowd and most of the fielders applauded his 50 warmly. The next ball was short – Bashy hooked strongly and it sailed high over the fielder on the boundary for a big six. Julian stood and stared angrily with his hands on his hips. He tore in to bowl again... Bashy drove through the covers on the up – four more.

The next was hammered over square leg for another boundary. Julian brought the field in for the fifth ball but he couldn't stop Bashy nudging it into a gap for the single. That left Cuthbert with one to face. He puffed out his chest as the big fast bowler raced in. It was probably the fastest delivery the young lad had ever seen in his life.

As the ball hammered into Cuthbert's boot, Bashy knew it was out. The whole of *Grand Bay* appealed for *lbw* and the umpire nodded and raised his finger. 118 for 9, said the score board – but it was really 118 all out.

Not enough, thought Bashy. Not nearly enough.

Bashy set off on the long walk towards the pavilion. They surely had no chance of defending such a small total.

The dream of playing in Trinidad was over. Then he stopped. On the boundary he saw someone waving and trying to do up his pads at the same time. It was Natty. Natty had arrived! He wasn't wearing his cricket gear – just a T-shirt and dark blue cargo shorts – but he was going to bat. Suddenly *Calypso* had a chance. What did they need? 180? 150 would be good, particularly after 27 for five.

Natty walked out to the middle, pulling on his batting gloves. "Sorry I late, Captain," he said casually, as if he'd just missed the bus.

Bashy gave him a gentle tap on the shoulder. "Last wicket stand," he said. "Make it count, man."

"What the bowling like?"

"Fast and straight. Get your eye in. Then we have some fun."

With a punch of their gloves Natty and Bashy set off to opposite ends of the wicket. Bashy was on strike. With the field back on the boundary, there were singles everywhere. Bashy decided to put his trust in Natty and he nudged the ball down and ran. Natty played out the rest of the over calmly – getting his eye in as his captain had told him.

But the *Grand Bay* fielders had already got the message. This boy, they'd taken for a last-minute stand-in, was no tail-ender. They were up against a class batter.

Chapter 10

In Constantine Bay, trouble was brewing. Diabolo burst on stage dressed as the Devil himself: red tights, red cloak, goatie beard and a pair of horns sticking through his bonnet. He was holding aloft a mighty trident as he launched into his song:

Last year the judges put me down
When they hand a pussy-cat the crown,
But tell him Diabolo back in town
And I mean to stand me ground.
'Cause I ain't 'fraid no black cat,
Diabolo ain't no mouse.
Diabolo go bring down the house
And knock the audience flat.

Everyone knew who the 'black cat' was. Pantha himself was nowhere to be seen, but his fans started booing. Their jeers only spurred Diabolo on. With a sly grin, he provoked his own cheering supporters by stabbing his trident in their direction as he sang:

Yes, my friends, just between you and me,
My lyrics will reveal with certainty
That under that Panama hat
The Growling Pantha is a pussy-cat.

With the words 'Pantha is a pussy-cat', fighting broke out in the crowd. Some of the fans had been drinking hard and they started throwing bottles. Banners were tossed into the air like battle standards as the Diabolo and Pantha supporters surged towards each other. Riccardo saw Snapper marshalling the fighters, driving them on like a general on the battlefield – only he seemed to be taking great care not to put himself in any danger. Brian and K-man, ahead of him, were swinging baseball bats over their heads. They'd come for trouble and they were finding it. A banner was thrown on to the stage but Diabolo sang on, revelling in the chaos.

> But tell him Diabolo back in town
> And I mean to stand me ground...

And then something happened. A ripple of laughter ran through a section of the crowd. You could hardly hear it at first over the roar of the fighting fans. But it grew, and people began pointing at the stage.

Riccardo craned his neck to see what they were looking at. It was a dog. A black dog. At first Riccardo thought it was a part of Diabolo's act. But he looked again and realised there was something familiar about the dog.

"Jessie," he gasped under his breath. Diabolo sang on, but he began to hesitate and look puzzled as the laughter grew louder.

'Cause I ain't 'fraid... no black cat
Diabolo... ain't no mouse.

Jessie trotted casually towards the front of the stage, saw Diabolo and decided to see if he had anything tasty to offer. The fighting had now stopped and the whole crowd, except for the Diabolo supporters, was rocking with laughter. Closer and closer came Jessie and as Diabolo sang 'Diabolo go bring down the house', she pushed her nose under the red gown right into the Devil's bum.

The song ended with a sharp squeal, as Diabolo lifted off the stage faster than Pantha's rocket. With a puzzled look, Jessie watched him land in a heap in front of her. Then she barked. Her nose was close to the microphone and the bark echoed round the bay. The crowd burst into applause.

When he saw the dog, Diabolo went wild. He aimed a kick at Jessie but she was too quick for him. He chased her across the stage, losing his bonnet and his horns, but she eluded him and ran back to the front as if to take a bow.

It was all over for Diabolo. The crowd booed as he hurled himself at the dog again and cheered when he kicked out at thin air and fell over once more. Finally, Jessie decided she'd had enough of the limelight and trotted calmly off the stage, pursued by the ridiculed figure of Diabolo.

"Diabolo ain't 'fraid black cat but he no match for you black dog, Ricky," said Martha. The girls, who had been watching Jessie's antics alongside Riccardo, were shaking with laughter, tears rolling down their cheeks.

"Did you train him to do that, Rikki?" giggled Millie.

"Diabolo face a picture," said Janine, recovering at last. "He never go on stage again after that humiliation."

"Only three to beat now, Butter-Finger," said Martha, struggling to be more serious. "You the front runner, brother, believe me."

"Definitely," said Millie. "Mind you, that girl QueeAnB sing well. She the one I feared of most." QueeAnB had wriggled her way through a rocking crowd-pleaser entitled 'Calypso dipso'. Her huge voice and performance got the audience bouncing and they'd given her a deafening send-off as she left the stage.

Diabolo was not seen again. The older people in the crowd were tutting and muttering – none of them could remember a contestant ever walking out in the middle of a Calypso Final. Some added that even if Diabolo hadn't retired, the judges would have been forced to disqualify him. His fans melted away, too, including Snapper and his mates.

The remaining four calypsonians drew lots for the second round. Riccardo picked a three. He was relieved not to be first on because he needed a few moments to rehearse the new song he'd written by the roadside. Millie, Martha and Janine were standing over him anxiously waiting for him to put the last touches to it – learning the chorus as he wrote…

The man in the shiny suit came back on stage to announce, to more boos and catcalls, the order of performance for round two:

> Roti Boy
> Pantha
> Butter-Finger
> QueeAnB

Chapter 11

Back at the Oval it was tea-time and the *Calypso* players were looking a lot happier. Bashy and Natty had put on 49 together – taking their chances and riding their luck. With the crowd cheering every run, the *Grand Bay* fielders soon lost their swagger. They were chased to all corners of the ground by the two *Calypso* stars with their bats blazing.

But the romp had to come to an end sooner or later... and finally Bashy edged to the keeper. It was the faintest snick, but he walked before the fielders could appeal. He'd scored 86. Natty was 23 not out. 167 – the *Calypso* total – was no more than average but the scale of the recovery had been amazing. The *Grand Bay* team ate their tea in silence.

When the Carriacou innings began, Natty made his mark immediately – he had the opener caught in the slips in his first over. But then disaster struck. Bashy was standing up to the stumps to Natty's bowling. A short-pitched ball was fired down the leg side and the batter swung late just as it thudded into the keeper's gloves. The bat caught Bashy a sickening blow on the right arm and he dropped the ball with a cry of pain.

He peeled off his glove and grabbed his wrist. It was swelling fast and his right hand was numb. Try as he might, he could scarcely move his fingers. Keeping wicket was out of the question.

"I'll do it," said Desmond, who was limping painfully and looking for an excuse to stop fielding.

"You ever keep wicket before?" asked Bashy.

"Well, er, no. But I field in the slips, man – same thing."

Bashy frowned. He'd have preferred to hand over to Natty. But with Natty bowling he had no choice, and Desmond put on the gloves. The result was every bit as bad as he feared. The first ball went through Desmond's legs for four byes. Fumbling and juggling, Desmond seemed to tie himself in knots and, after he'd let through another four byes, Bashy posted a long stop. With more runs coming from the keeper's mistakes than off the bat, Bashy had to do something quick to stop the rot. But what? His wrist was so painful, he could barely keep his mind on the game.

Julian, the *Grand Bay* captain, led the charge. Rohan went for 12 runs off his first over, not counting the byes, and, although Natty bowled tightly and took a sharp return catch to dismiss the other opener, the visitors were soon galloping towards an easy victory.

Leo came out with drinks and gave Ryan and Rohan some much-needed fast-bowling advice. Meanwhile, Bashy decided to change keepers again and Desmond gave up the gloves rather grumpily to Natty.

Moments later, Desmond added further to his captain's woes. Natty chased after a leg bye and threw down the stumps on the turn. The batter was well out of his ground and, while Natty celebrated the wicket, Desmond, backing up the throw, ran straight into Cuthbert. He went right over the top of him and performed a spectacular mid-air somersault. When he stood up, his bad leg gave way completely and he had to be helped off the pitch.

Reduced to ten men again, Bashy went even further on the defensive. Ryan and Rohan were both bowling a better line and the run flow slowed. But not enough. A delicate leg glide brought up Julian's 50. It had been a chanceless performance and all the *Calypso* players applauded sportingly. At 123 for three, Bashy's only hope lay in taking quick wickets. But who could he turn to? It was time for a gamble and he threw the ball to little Cuthbert.

"Give it plenty air, man. Toss it up," he told the diminutive leg spinner.

"And plenty spin," said Cuthbert, with the confidence of a seasoned pro. Bashy caught sight of the looks on some of the fielders' faces. He, too, knew it was a big ask for a young kid to bowl at a top batter who was seeing the ball like a breadfruit and had just posted 50.

Cuthbert's first ball was short and Julian coshed it dismissively for four. The next was a slow, full toss, which disappeared one bounce over the mid-on boundary. Bashy clapped his hands in frustration and looked over towards the bowler but decided to say nothing. Cuthbert still seemed calm enough. He tossed a catch to himself and ran in. The ball looped and dipped and Julian drove off the front foot. The snick was heard all round the ground, and Natty behind the stumps knocked up the ball and took the catch at the second attempt. Cuthbert jumped for joy and nearly leapt into Bashy's arms. He had grabbed the big wicket.

The *Calypso* players swarmed around to

congratulate him as Julian walked slowly off. Bashy did his sums. If nothing else, it took his mind off the painful throb in his wrist. *Grand Bay* needed 37 runs to win at less than four runs an over and the odds were still firmly stacked in their favour. But with a new batter at the crease, there was at least a glimmer of hope.

Chapter 12

A sharp squall of rain passed over Constantine Bay. It was met with a sea of umbrellas. Moments later the sun appeared again and Riccardo walked out on stage.

This time he had the crowd behind him from the word go. *Butter-Finger, Butter-Finger,* they chanted. He was still feeling very nervous, but he didn't trip over his feet or knock over the mike. Someone shouted, "Where your black dog, Butter-Finger?" and they all laughed. Word had got around that Jessie belonged to Riccardo.

The girls joined him at the front of the stage and took a bow. This time there were no costumes or dance steps. They stood alongside Butter-Finger in their denim skirts and jackets, Martha on his left, Janine and Millie to his right.

"One, two, three ..." said Martha into her mike, and they began. Riccardo sang his song fiercely, half-wishing that Snapper and Co were still in the audience to hear it.

> Carnival is bacchanal,
> Free-up time for one and all.
> It time to move your feet
> When the beat so sweet
> And the steel band call.
>
> The sun beating down
> On the black, the white, the brown,
> Hugging-up taking place all over town.
> Rhythm giving birth to emotion,
> Belly and back in one flowing ocean.

The Constantine Bay crowd swayed and cheered. Martha, Millie and Janine jumped down from the stage and sang with the crowd. "Hugging-up taking place all over town," they sang, hugging everyone as they went – black, brown and white.

Riccardo's calypso was the spark that lit the fire. It was what everyone had been waiting for. The fans applauded and stamped and whistled as he took his bow. They dragged him back for more and he sang another verse for them:

> The sun beating down
> On the black, the white, the brown,
> Bodies moving to one horizon
> And sweetness sounding out of iron.
> No slowing down till Ash Wednesday come.

Encouraged by the girls waving their arms, the crowd joined in the chorus, snaking and wining and flinging themselves in the air.

"Monarch Butter-Finger!" shouted an old woman with a voice like a foghorn. And Riccardo, Martha, Millie and Janine finally danced off stage to deafening applause and stamping and whistling.

Pantha's and Roti Boy's songs had been well received, but both had lacked that special something the crowd was longing for. Roti Boy had been a bit unlucky that the sound system had started making funny, high-pitched noises during his song. But now, at last, the jump-up was in full swing. And when QueeAnB hit the stage in a skimpy dress, jiving to the all-girl steel pan band, she was met by a wall of noise. Her saucy dance went on for several bars before the song began.

It was a raunchy catwalk routine and she encouraged two or three of the best male dancers from
the crowd to join her on stage. And then she sang:

> Work it, girl,
> Shake it,
> Even if you
> Have to fake it.

> Wave your hand
> In the air,
> QueeAnB got de
> Sting in she tail;
> So boys, mind your stumps,
> QueeAnB go
> Knock off your bail,
> And when she start to flow
> Tell me how you like it
> When the ball keep low.

> Boys, I don't mean to tease,
> But I reversing my swing
> And bouncing as I please;
> Yes, I like it when you
> Play cross my line.

That is when QueeAnB
Does strut she shine,
Tell me when last you see
A cricket ball wine.

So work it, girl,
Shake it
Even if you
Have to fake it.

QueeAnB jumped down and wriggled and danced with the fans at the front until she could sing no more. When she finally appeared back on stage, she got the biggest cheer of the day. "The crowd go riot if she don't win," Riccardo said to Martha.

"But that not calypso," insisted Janine, "Girl singing a rumba rhythm or something. Sure as hell not calypso."

"Don't care what it called. It got me movin'," said Millie.

"Janine right. You can't give calypso crown to rumba queen," said Martha.

The panel of five judges didn't keep the crowd waiting for long. The four calypsonians paraded back on stage. Riccardo stood on the right of the group next to QueeAnB. The Monarch's throne was placed in the centre in front of them. One by one the judges cast their votes in a hat placed on the throne. Then the results were called out.

"Butter-Finger, two votes," shouted the man with the shiny suit. "And QueeAnB ...... THREE VOTES!"

There were a few boos, quickly drowned out by the hooting horns and whistles and stamping.

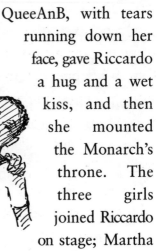

QueeAnB, with tears running down her face, gave Riccardo a hug and a wet kiss, and then she mounted the Monarch's throne. The three girls joined Riccardo on stage; Martha put a sisterly arm round him as they all applauded the new Monarch.

"You sang the best, Ricky, believe me. You should have won. Those three judges too mean to vote for a young boy like you," she said.

Riccardo smiled. What could he say – that he didn't care? That coming second was way beyond his wildest dreams? Just a few hours ago, when he didn't have a calypso to sing, he had been facing humiliation. And now, hadn't he beaten the Growling Pantha?

But Martha wasn't the only person to tell him he should have won. Some of the older spectators, including his Uncle Alvin, argued long into the night about whether the winning song had been a true calypso.

QueeAnB stopped sobbing and rose majestically from the throne to sing her song again. Count Crawfish appeared from nowhere at Riccardo's side and shouted in his ear, "That calypso the best you ever write, Rikki Tikki. I proud of you."

"Sexy song beat me good," said Riccardo, smiling.

"Always the way," said Crawfish. "Now, you take a bow with Missy Q and we go see how you cricket team faring."

The game! Riccardo was ashamed to admit that he'd forgotten all about it.

Chapter 13

Count Crawfish and Riccardo rode to the Oval on the back of a flat-bed motor trailer with the Sweet Pan band, the most famous steel drum band on the Island. It was like a victory parade. People ran alongside the truck, snaking through the streets and calling for Butter-Finger to sing his song. The pan drummers took up the tune:

> Carnival is bacchanal,
> Free-up time for one and all.
> It time to move your feet
> When the beat so sweet
> And the steel band call.

Riccardo sang the song right through once on his own, and then Count Crawfish joined him in front of the band. By the time the cavalcade reached the Oval, hundreds of people were chanting Riccardo's words. The crowd poured into the ground and Riccardo jumped off the trailer and battled his way towards the pavilion.

Through the excited throng he spotted Ryan on the pitch. *Calypso* were fielding. What was the score?

His first glimpse of the scoreboard told him that the game had reached crisis point. 160 for five. How many overs left? Two. *Grand Bay* needed just eight to win off 12 balls. Plenty of wickets in hand. A very small boy was bowling slow loopy leg spin. Riccardo guessed it was Cuthbert.

"*Calypso!* Give it the beat!" shouted Riccardo. But he knew that all *Grand Bay* needed to do was to push the singles and they would win easily. He watched the batter take a huge swing at another tempting slow delivery from tiny Cuthbert. He missed, and turned to see that Natty had whipped off the bails. He was out – stumped.

Riccardo leapt up and down, cheering wildly. But why was Natty keeping wicket, he wondered? What was Bashy doing fielding at extra-cover?

Bashy clapped his hands together to spur on the team, and winced. He'd forgotten about his injured wrist. As he looked over to the scoreboard, he saw Riccardo. "You fielding, man. Come on!" he yelled.

Riccardo couldn't hear. He waved back at Bashy. Then he caught sight of Desmond, sitting with his foot up by the pavilion.

Desmond pointed to the ice pack strapped to his leg, "Butter-Finger – substitute. Get out there."

Riccardo got the message at last. *Calypso* were a fielder short. He ran on to the field but the umpire told him he'd have to wait until the end of the over. So he stood anxiously on the boundary, watching.

Cuthbert bowled. The new batter missed and Natty watched the ball miss the stumps by a whisker and groaned.

"Spin to win!" Riccardo shouted.

Cuthbert was turning the ball a long way and luckily, the batter was still trying to slog him for four. Ball after ball evaded the bat until the very last delivery, when a lucky top edge bounced away for a boundary.

Four to win, and Rohan to bowl the last over. Riccardo raced on to the pitch. He'd used up all his nerves at the Final. Now he was focused and determined. He didn't even hear the cheers of the crowd.

"Deep mid-wicket!" shouted Bashy, and Riccardo took up his position on the boundary. The pressure built up. Rohan had a huge appeal for *lbw* turned down and then went past the bat for another dot ball. The third ball was swatted away to square leg, and Natty made a great stop on the boundary to save a four and the match – but they still ran two. With only two needed for victory, the new batter went for a suicidal single and Ravi picked up and threw down the wicket with a direct hit. Out! 166 for seven.

As the next batsman walked to the wicket Bashy had a brief discussion with the umpire. Then he ran round to speak to every fielder. Riccardo walked in from the boundary to hear what he had to say.

"Two balls left, but they only need one run. If the scores level, they win."

"Why?" asked Riccardo.

"They only lost seven wickets – if it's a tie, the wickets count for them."

"They still slogging."

"I know. P'raps they don't know only one

needed. Got to stop the single, but you stay on boundary for the catch."

"Don't worry, Bash. We going to win," said Riccardo.

Rohan ran in again and the batter swung wildly – a thick top edge – and up and up went the ball. Riccardo saw it immediately, and ran in to meet it.

Whoa! It was going up a long, long way. Bashy was off the mark too, racing out from square leg by the umpire. "Mine!" he cried. Riccardo was still looking up at the ball which was now descending very fast. He put on the brakes, but he tripped over his own feet and went sprawling … right in Bashy's path. Bashy, looking up at the ball, hadn't seen Riccardo. His foot caught him a glancing blow on the side of the head. The captain stumbled, but somehow kept his balance. He still had the ball in his sights. It struck the palm of his right hand. There was a stab of pain. He couldn't close his fingers on it. The ball hit his knee and lobbed forward in the air.

Riccardo had a fraction of a second to act. He lurched sideways, stuck out his hand and the ball settled snugly in his palm.

Bashy stared at him for a second in amazement.

Rohan was the first to react. "That's out, man. Out! Out! Out!" he kept yelling.

"Supersub Butter-Finger!" said Bashy, pulling Riccardo to his feet and giving him a big hug. But it wasn't time for celebrations yet. There was still one delivery to go. Bashy grabbed the ball and ran towards Rohan and, as the new batter made his way slowly to the middle, he carefully adjusted his field. The batsman took guard and Bashy moved his field again.

Now everyone, including Riccardo, was in close to save the single. Whatever happened, the batters would run. All the fielders were on their toes, walking in as Rohan bowled. The batter swung, missed and ran, dropping his bat as he scampered down the wicket. The ball flashed through to Natty who hurled it back at the stumps... and missed. Rohan was following through; he snatched up the ball on the run and threw underarm. Over went the middle stump ... knocked flat.

"Howzat!" screamed eleven players.

The umpire didn't hesitate. "Out." Up went the finger for the run-out.

Chapter 14

By now the crowd was enormous, dancing to the pan bands in the big stand and under the palm trees. With the fall of the final wicket they poured on to the pitch. More and more revellers were flowing in from Constantine Bay and from all over the Island as the news spread that the big jump-up was happening at the Oval. In front of the pavilion *Calypso*'s band played 'Bat and Ball' and the pan drummers round the ground took up the tune.

> Today Bat and Ball will meet
> In a sweet calypso beat.
>
> Batsman, beat the shine,
> Bowler, find your line.
> When the band begin to play
> Bat and Ball will break away.

Leaving the pitch, the players had to dodge through a melée of cheering supporters who were none too gentle with their back-slapping and hugging. Riccardo was hoisted up on the shoulders of two big revellers before he finally escaped to the safety of the pavilion. One of the umpires was knocked to the ground, losing the three stumps he was carrying and his hat.

"Lucky no one get badly hurt out there," said Bashy, slumping down on a bench in the changing room. He spotted Riccardo and looked suddenly embarrassed. "Hey, man, I forgot to ask… "

"I come second," Riccardo beamed.

"Second! Congratulations, man," said Ravi.

"Who beat you?" asked Leo. "Pantha, I bet."

"No, QueeAnB."

"What! They vote for a woman?" said Leo.

"And what wrong with that, Big Lug?" said Desmond. "She a good singer. Pity she beat Butter-Finger, though."

"When we going to hear your new songs, Riccardo?" asked Bashy.

Riccardo was about to answer when Natty walked in. All heads turned towards him.

"Where you been hiding, man?" said Bashy, finally putting the question that was on everyone's lips.

"Talking to my ma," said Natty sheepishly.

"She not too happy."

"I mean, where you been these last two days?"

"That what she asking me," said Natty. "Can't understand why everyone getting so excited. I ain't been to the moon."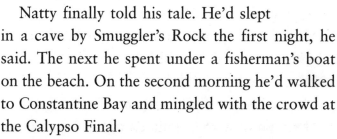

"You going to tell us, or I smacking you?" said Leo.

Natty finally told his tale. He'd slept in a cave by Smuggler's Rock the first night, he said. The next he spent under a fisherman's boat on the beach. On the second morning he'd walked to Constantine Bay and mingled with the crowd at the Calypso Final.

"So why you been playing hide-and-seek all this time?" said Leo.

"Man, if I tell you, you going to laugh at me," said Natty.

"No, man, we ain't going to laugh," insisted Leo.

"It 'cause I 'fraid of flying," said Natty in a quiet voice.

Leo snorted with laughter. "You joking."

"If man supposed to fly, God give him wings," said Natty.

The players stared at him blankly, and then slowly the truth began to dawn. "Flying to Trinidad?" said Bashy.

Natty nodded. "I never go on no airplane. The more I think about it, the worse it get. And soon I can't think about nothing else. I rather miss the big final than face that plane."

"That stupid," said Leo.

"No it ain't," insisted Riccardo. "Everybody know what you like when you see a dog coming."

"It ain't the same."

"It is," said Bashy. "If a dog walk in here, you jump out the window."

Leo looked away sulkily.

"My dad won't fly on airplanes," said Ravi.

"I try not to think about flying, but everything going wrong," continued Natty. "Batting, bowling, captaining. It like a big weight on my shoulders. Then I don't want to captain any more and in the end I run away."

"We look for you all over," said Bashy.

"Under that boat, I thinking all the time about the game," said Natty. "I want to play but I say to myself, what will happen if we win? I have to go on plane to Trinidad. And then at Calypso Final I see Butter-Finger. I watch you standing on stage,

126

Riccardo. And I see you scared as hell."

"When I fall over that microphone, I want to die, man," said Riccardo.

"But you sing like a bird. And I say to myself, Natty, look... he ain't hiding away from trouble like you. Butter-Finger ain't no coward. *Heaven is for real on a cricket ground*, you sing. And when I hear them words, I know it time to stand up for myself and for *Calypso*. And if we win, I fly on the plane. And I sit next to Butter-Finger."

"Lucky for us you play. Without you we get beat, for sure," said Bashy.

"No way. Team performance come through. You batting, Cuthbert bowling and Riccardo catching."

Everyone laughed. "True 'nough," said Bashy. "But I telling you, this ain't no easy team to captain. I glad to hand them back to you, Natty man."

◉ ◉ ◉

The presentation ceremony was held in front of the pavilion. *Calypso*'s players joined the *Grand Bay* team. The band was still playing but now there was a trio of singers: Wesley and Count

Crawfish had been joined by the new Calypso Monarch, QueeAnB. Horns sounded and children ran about throwing taped-up tennis balls in the air.

The smell of goat curry and dhal puri mingled with the whiff of paraffin from the stoves. Riccardo glimped Jessie winding her way optimistically amongst the revellers, tail wagging, her nose expertly picking out the best of the cooking smells. The unsung hero of the Calypso Final, who had saved the day from a riot, was back to her usual tricks. She grabbed a hot chicken leg and, with a yelp, half-triumph, half-pain, bounded off, pursued by a fat woman in a white apron.

The two captains were presented to the crowd. As the applause died down Jessie bounded across in front of them, the fat owner of the chicken still in hot pursuit. *Dog eat champion, Dog eat champion,* came the chant from those who had witnessed Jessie's earlier performance.

At last, Bashy was voted Man of the Match for his outstanding innings and Bashy and Julian made short speeches about what a good close contest it had been. Then, to loud cheers, the jump-up began again. Riccardo, with Martha and Millie and Janine, joined Wesley, Crawfish and QueeAnB and they sang the newly-crowned Monarch's song as she wriggled and cavorted up and down the steps of the pavilion. Natty and Bashy and the whole *Calypso* CC team linked arms behind them and joined in the chorus.

As the cheers died down, Riccardo stepped forward boldly. A new song was running through his head. He'd come a long way from the days when everyone laughed at him because he couldn't bat and he couldn't catch. And he owed it all to calypso and his love of words. And to cricket. Crawfish was right – the words come when the mood is right. It was time for him to sing his song:

Cricket is a game of glorious uncertainty
But it certainly improve your vocabulary.
Butter-Finger say, and I'm sure you'll agree,

That cricket commentary is a friend of poetry.
This language is yours, this language is mine,
Cricket gives the poet in you a chance to shine.

The other day I turned on my radio
And the commentator was in full flow.
He described a stroke as agricultural
And one yorker was positively lethal.
I hear the open field was free acreage
For the batsman to go on the rampage.
I had to smile how he using the language.

Yes, this game of glorious uncertainty
Can certainly improve your vocabulary.
Butter-Finger say, and I'm sure you'll agree,
That cricket commentary is a friend of poetry.
This language is yours, this language is mine
Cricket gives the poet in you a chance to shine.

That commentator caught my ears attentively
When he said certain overs were mandatory,
And when the batsman slog out like a brute
I hear how the ball took the aerial route.
I couldn't deny he was speaking the truth,
But when he mentioned low trajectory,
Man, I had to reach for the dictionary.

Butter-Finger say, and I'm sure you'll agree,
That cricket commentary is a friend of poetry.
This language is yours, this language is mine,
Cricket gives the poet in you a chance to shine.
Before you know, you bouncing words on a line.
Yes, Butter-Finger say sing it one more time:
Cricket gives the poet in you a chance to shine!

Bob Cattell has been a cricket fan all his life and a supporter of the England team through thick and thin. He worked as a bookseller for many years and is now a writer of children's books, best known for his Glory Gardens and Strikers series about cricket and football. *Butter-Finger*, his first book with John Agard for Frances Lincoln, won a WOW! Award in 2006. Bob lives near Southwold, Suffolk.

John Agard is one of the most
popular poets writing in Britain today.
His collection for young children,
We Animals Would Like A Word With You,
illustrated by Satoshi Kitamura, won a
Smarties Bronze Award, and he is the author of
the much-loved *Brer Rabbit and the Tug of War*,
illustrated by Korky Paul,
and *Wriggle Piggy Toes* with Jenny Bent.
He lives in Lewes, Sussex with his partner,
the poet Grace Nichols.

BUTTER-FINGER
Bob Cattell and John Agard
Illustrated by Pam Smy

Riccardo Small may not be a great cricketer –
he's only played twice before for *Calypso Cricket
Club* – but he's mad about the game and can tell you
the averages of every West Indies cricketer in history.
His other love is writing calypsos.
Today is Riccardo's chance to make his mark
with *Calypso CC* against The Saints.
The game goes right down to the wire with captain,
Natty and team-mates, Bashy and Leo striving for
victory, but then comes the moment
that changes everything for Riccardo...

ISBN 978-1-84507-376-3

THE GREAT TUG OF WAR
Beverley Naidoo
Illustrated by Piet Grobler

Mmutla the hare is a mischievous trickster.
When Tswhene the baboon is vowing to throw you
off a cliff, you need all the tricks you can think of!
When Mmutla tricks Tlou the elephant
and Kubu the hippo into having an epic tug-of-war,
the whole savanna is soon laughing at their
foolishness. However, small animals should not
make fun of big animals and King Lion sets out
to teach cheeky little Mmutla a lesson...

These tales are the African origins of America's
beloved stories of Brer Rabbit. Their warm humour
is guaranteed to enchant new readers of all ages.

ISBN 978-1-84507-055-7

PURPLE CLASS AND THE SKELINGTON
Sean Taylor
Illustrated by Helen Bate
Cover illustrated by Polly Dunbar

Meet Purple Class – there is Jamal who often forgets
his reading book, Ivette who is the best in the class
at everything, Yasmin who is sick on every school trip,
Jodie who owns a crazy snake called Slinkypants,
Leon who is great at rope-swinging,
Shea who knows all about blood-sucking slugs
and Zina who makes a rather disturbing discovery
in the teacher's chair…

Has Mr Wellington died? Purple Class is sure
he must have done when they find a skeleton
sitting in his chair. Is this Mr Wellington's skelington?
What will they say to the school inspector?
Featuring a calamitous cast of classmates,
the adventures of Purple Class will make you
laugh out loud in delight.

ISBN 978-1-84507-377-0

PURPLE CLASS AND THE FLYING SPIDER
Sean Taylor
Illustrated by Helen Bate
Cover illustrated by Polly Dunbar

Purple Class are back in four new school stories!
Leon has managed to lose 30 violins,
much to the horror of the violin teacher;
Jodie thinks she has uncovered an unexploded bomb
in the vegetable patch; Shea has allowed Bad Boy,
Purple Class's guinea pig to escape;
and Ivette has discovered a scary flying spider,
just in time for Parent's Evening!

ISBN 978-1-84507-627-6

GHADDAR THE GHOUL
and other Palestinian Stories
Sonia Nimr
Introduction by Ghada Karmi
Illustrated by Hannah Shaw

Why do Snakes eat Frogs?
What makes a Ghoul turn Vegetarian?
How can a Woman make a Bored Prince Smile?
The answers can be found in this delicious
anthology of Palestinian folk stories.
A wry sense of humour runs through their cast
of characterful women, genial tricksters
and mischievous animals.
Sonia Nimr's upbeat storytelling,
bubbling with wit and humour,
will delight readers discovering for the first time
the rich tradition of Palestinian storytelling.

ISBN 978-1-84507-523-1

THE PRINCE WHO THOUGHT
HE WAS A ROOSTER
and other Jewish Stories
Ann Jungman
Introduction by Michael Rosen
Illustrated by Sarah Adams

A Chilli Champion?… a Golem?…
a Prince who thinks he's a Rooster?
Find them all in this collection of traditional
Jewish tales – lovingly treasured, retold and carried
through countries as far apart as Poland, Tunisia,
Czechoslovakia, Morocco, Russia and Germany,
with a cast of eccentric princes, flustered tailors,
wise rabbis and the oldest champion of all!
Seasoned with wit, humour and magic,
Ann Jungman's retellings of stories familiar
to Jewish readers are sure to delight
a new, wider readership.

ISBN 978-1-84507-794-5

ROAR, BULL, ROAR!
Andrew Fusek Peters and Polly Peters
Illustrated by Anke Weckmann

What is the real story of the ghostly Roaring Bull?
Who is the batty old lady in the tattered clothes?
Why is the new landlord such a nasty piece of work?

Czech brother and sister Jan and Marie arrive in
rural England in the middle of the night – and not
everyone is welcoming. As they try to settle into
their new school, they are plunged into
a series of mysteries. Old legends are revived
as Jan and Marie unearth shady secrets in
a desperate bid to save their family from eviction.
In their quest, they find unlikely allies
and deadly enemies – who will stop at nothing
to keep the past buried.

ISBN 978-1-84507-520-0

MIXING IT
Rosemary Hayes

Fatimah is a devout Muslim. Steve is a regular guy
who has never given much thought to faith.
Both happen to be in the same street the day
a terrorist bomb explodes. Steve is badly injured
and when the emergency services arrive,
Fatimah has bandaged his shattered leg and is
cradling his head in her lap, willing him to stay alive.
But the Press is there too, and their picture
makes the front page of every newspaper.
'Love across the divide,' scream the headlines.
Then the anonymous 'phone calls start.
Can Steve and Fatimah rise above the hatred
and learn to understand each other?
But while they are breaking down barriers,
the terrorists have another target in mind...

ISBN 978-1-84507-495-1

GIVE ME SHELTER
Stories about children seeking asylum
Edited by Tony Bradman

Sabine is escaping a civil war...
Danny doesn't want to be soldier...
What has happened to Samir's family?

Here is a collection of stories about children from
all over the world who must leave their
homes and families behind to seek a new life
in a strange land. Many are escaping war
or persecution. All must become asylum seekers
in the free lands of the West.
If they do not escape, they will not survive.

These stories, some written by asylum seekers
and people who work closely with them,
are about our humanity and the fight for
the most basic of our rights – to live.
They are testimony to all the people in need of
shelter and those from safer countries who
act with sympathy and understanding.

ISBN 978-1-84507-522-4

LINES IN THE SAND
New Writing on War and Peace
Edited by Mary Hoffman
and Rhiannon Lassiter

Talented writers and illustrators from all over
the world have come together to produce this book.
They were inspired by their feelings about the
conflict in Iraq, though the wars covered in this
collection range from a 13th-century Crusade through
the earlier wars of the 20th century to recent conflicts
in Nigeria, the Falklands, Kosovo and South Africa,
right up to what was happening in Iraq in 2003.

With over one hundred and fifty poems,
stories and pictures about war and peace,
Lines in the Sand offers hope for the future.

All profits and royalties to UNICEF

ISBN 978-0-7112-2282-7